One Perfect Boy
Text copyright © 2012 by Kathy Samuels
Illustrations copyright © by Richard L. Marks

ISBN-13 978-0615957234

Progeny Quest Publishers
Printed in the U.S.A.

One
Perfect
Boy

This book is dedicated to women everywhere; those who have had the joy of raising children,
women who have never had children of their own, but have loved the children God has placed in their lives,
and those women who grieve over the loss of their children through abortion, miscarriage,
SIDS, illness, tragedy, or broken relationships.
You are loved; and my prayer is that you will receive
Jesus' gift of unconditional love for you.
-*Kathy Samuels*

Dear Reader

While reading scripture one morning a few years ago, I began to wonder about Jesus' childhood and at that moment, this story was born in my heart. Of course this is fiction, as very little is known about Jesus' life between his miraculous birth and the beginning of his ministry nearly thirty years later. This story includes imaginary characters as well as known people in the Bible who walked and talked with Jesus.

How exciting it was for me as I searched for possibilities of Jesus' childhood in the Bible!

As you turn each page, imagine peeking through a window of time for a glimpse of what Jesus' childhood might have been. My prayer is that as you journey through this little book, God will plant in your heart a desire to search the scriptures, and that you will love Jesus more after reading One Perfect Boy.

—*Kathy Samuels*

My hope for this book is that many will realize Jesus is real. He actually grew up and walked the earth as a man. He was tempted in every way that you and I are yet without sin, and He can relate to anything you could ever go through. He is the savior of the world and died on a cross for you and me.

We can have eternal life with Him if we admit we are sinners and cry out to Him to save us. Jesus is Lord!

-*Rich Marks*

The road to Egypt was long and dusty but baby Jesus felt safe and cozy snuggled close to his mother as they swayed gently on the donkey's back. He giggled when her kisses tickled his tummy and his little fat feet. But then she softly ran her fingers through the fine hair on his head and his little ears tuned in to the sound of his mother's heartbeat. His blinks became long and slow, and he drifted into a peaceful sleep.

Joseph held the donkey's rope and hummed a tune to the clip-clop of hoof-beats. Mary squinted through the rising heat, and took a grateful breath as village rooftops and trees appeared in the distance. "Look, Joseph," Mary said quietly. Joseph shaded his eyes from the sun and looked across the desert. Then he turned toward her and smiled. Their long journey from Bethlehem was almost over.

And just like you
As children do,
Jesus grew!

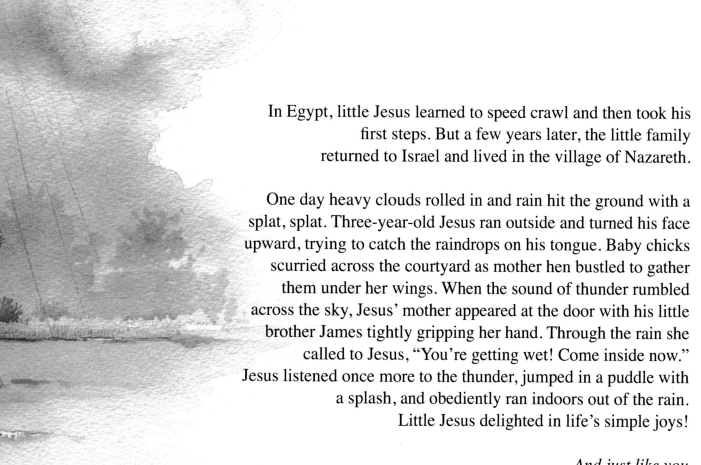

In Egypt, little Jesus learned to speed crawl and then took his first steps. But a few years later, the little family returned to Israel and lived in the village of Nazareth.

One day heavy clouds rolled in and rain hit the ground with a splat, splat. Three-year-old Jesus ran outside and turned his face upward, trying to catch the raindrops on his tongue. Baby chicks scurried across the courtyard as mother hen bustled to gather them under her wings. When the sound of thunder rumbled across the sky, Jesus' mother appeared at the door with his little brother James tightly gripping her hand. Through the rain she called to Jesus, "You're getting wet! Come inside now." Jesus listened once more to the thunder, jumped in a puddle with a splash, and obediently ran indoors out of the rain. Little Jesus delighted in life's simple joys!

And just like you
As children do,
Jesus grew!

God had chosen Joseph to be Jesus' earthly father. Joseph was a carpenter. Five-year-old Jesus loved the smell of fresh-cut wood inside the carpenter shop. As sunshine streamed through the tiny window, he could see flecks of sawdust dancing in the air. Jesus stood near and watched closely as his father cut and shaped a beautiful piece of olive wood. The table he was making was almost finished.

His father asked for a tool and Jesus quickly handed him the right one. As Joseph worked, he said, "Let me hear you recite your verses from the Torah*." And Jesus could say them all perfectly! Joseph smiled and said, "Very good!" but Jesus was thinking, "If that table had ears and a brain, it would be the smartest table in Nazareth!" And he knew all there was to learn in the Torah and about making useful things of wood.

And just like you
As children do,
Jesus grew!

* *First five books of the bible*

Seven-year-old Jesus never missed a chance to run from his house up the hillside to Grandfather's house. At the door, Grandfather reached out with both arms and Jesus hugged his waist tightly. Then they walked from the house to the garden with Grandfather's tanned and weathered hand gently resting across Jesus' shoulder.

In the garden, they knelt together and dug into the soil, sometimes finding fat earthworms. Grandfather taught him how deep to plant the seeds and how to water without washing the seeds away. There was a grape vineyard too, and in early spring, Grandfather showed Jesus how to cut off branches so the vine would produce beautiful, healthy grapes.

After spending the morning together, Grandfather always gave him a rub on his head and a bag of almonds to take home. Jesus walked a way down the path and when he turned to look back, he could see Grandfather standing there, watching him go. They waved good-bye and down the hill he skipped, stopping along the way to pick a bunch of flowers to brighten his mother's table.

And just like you
As children do,
Jesus grew!

Every year when the flowers were blooming, all the Jewish families walked up to Jerusalem for Passover. On the last night of their journey, the families settled down together under the stars. Before they went to bed, Jesus' father gathered his family around him and pointed toward the twinkling city lights in the distance. "You see, children, the lights of a city cannot be hidden in the darkness," he said. "You can shine in the same way if you walk in the light of the Lord."

Then it was time for bed. Father tucked them in and Mother kissed each one. "Goodnight! I love you!" their voices mingled together. After a few minutes of silence, whispers were heard from the children and their father's stern voice came out of the dark, "Children, that's enough. Go to sleep." Suddenly, it was quiet under the covers and in the soft shadows of moonlight only the crickets were chirping.

Eight-year-old Jesus was the first one to be quiet and fall asleep.

And the next day…

They finally arrived outside the city of Jerusalem! While the grown-ups were setting up tents, the children found each other and escaped to play a blindfold game. While playing the first game, Jesus noticed a woman and a little boy sitting next to their tent. They were making clay out of mud and forming it into small shapes. Jesus ran over to them and said to the boy, "Come play the game with us!" The woman spoke kindly to Jesus, "My son was born blind and he can't run and play like other children." Then Jesus spoke to the blind boy, "You can play this game! Go wash the mud off your hands."

The mother helped him wash, and Jesus took the boy by his hand and led him toward the children. "He's going to play with us!" announced Jesus. Everyone except Jesus' new friend put on the blindfolds. Then the game began. Soon, all the children were begging to play with the blind boy because his team won every time! And Jesus saw the blind boy's mother watching from not very far away. She was smiling.

And just like you
As children do,
Jesus grew!

Back home in Nazareth, nine-year-old Jesus had a secret place where he liked to go when he needed to be alone. Well, not really alone, because he had long talks with his Heavenly Father in this secret place. He would lie on the grass and watch the leaves above him flutter in the breeze.

One day, Jesus noticed a nest near the top of the tree. He grabbed a low tree limb and pulled up with his strong arms. He braced his feet on the trunk and began to climb. Finally, he hugged a branch way up high and peeked inside the nest. Being very quiet and still, he counted the sky-blue eggs. "One…two…. three…four." Mother bird flew in and perched herself on a branch nearby. "Don't be afraid," Jesus said to the bird, and with a flutter of wings, she came to rest very near his face. She gave Jesus a curious look, hopped into her nest, fluffed her feathers, and softly settled over her eggs.

After watching mother bird for a moment, Jesus carefully climbed down from the tree, and when his feet touched the ground, he said, "Thank you, Father, for creating birds and caring for them." Then he jogged down the rocky path toward home. It was late afternoon and he knew his earthly father would soon be whistling for him and his brothers.

And just like you
As children do,
Jesus grew!

One day, Jesus woke up at sunrise and packed himself a lunch. Then he hurried out the door to join his shepherd friend on a hillside just outside Nazareth. Together they watched as woolly sheep nibbled on grass fresh with dew, and as the sunshine warmed the morning, they laughed at the frisky lambs kicking up their heels. Then the old shepherd picked up his rod and staff and called to the sheep. They raised their heads and followed as he led them to a greener pasture near a quiet stream.

Jesus stayed all day helping the shepherd, and in the evening they counted the sheep. "A little lamb is missing," said the shepherd, and they searched the rocky hillside. Ten-year-old Jesus quickly found the lost lamb on a steep cliff and carefully walked near the edge to pick her up. He lifted her securely over his shoulders, just as he had seen the shepherd do, and carried her back to safety.

The shepherd liked the days when Jesus came to help. This smart boy always seemed to know exactly where to find a lost lamb. When it was time to go home, Jesus said goodbye and headed down the hill toward the stream. He was quite smelly after a day with the sheep and he knew his mother wouldn't let him in the house unless he had washed.

And just like you
As children do,
Jesus grew!

Jesus' family left Nazareth early one bright morning and followed the road to the Sea of Galilee. They were meeting their friends Zebedee, his wife and their two boys, James and John. One night, as eleven-year-old Jesus was helping his father set up the tent, little brother Simon asked, "Are we there yet?" His father ruffled Simon's hair and said, "When you see the sea you'll know we're almost there."

The next day, as they came to the top of a hill, the sea came into view and the older boys raced down the hill! It wasn't long before they spotted their friends on the shore jumping and waving to them. Giving each other friendly slaps on the back they quickly jumped into the cool fresh water. They splashed and swam all afternoon while their parents watched from the shore. Jesus loved days like this, making memories with his family and friends.

And in the evening of that day…

The children were called to eat supper, and when everyone was there Zebedee asked the blessing. In that quiet moment they could hear the waves gently lapping on the shore. When they heard "Amen", they eagerly filled their baskets with bread, figs, olives and fresh fish that Zebedee had caught earlier in the day! Sitting down on blankets, rocks or small logs, they ate, and everyone agreed the meal was fit for a king!

As the two families sat around the campfire talking, laughing, and sharing their fish stories, dark clouds rolled in from across the sea. Lightning began to flash from the sky to earth and sounds of thunder rumbled in the distance, interrupting their story telling. Suddenly, a huge thunderclap crashed around them and sent the little ones screaming and scrambling to the safety of their parents' arms! But Jesus stood and turned toward the sea. He watched as his two friends, James and John, boldly rushed toward the storm; and like two ferocious lions, the boys roared back at the thunder! After a few seconds of shocked silence, everyone broke into laughter. The storm passed quickly, and the families told stories and sang around the campfire long into the night. And Jesus' voice, pure and clear, could be heard above all the others.

And just like you
As children do,
Jesus grew!

When Jesus was twelve he had grown as tall as his mother. He and his family were on another journey to Jerusalem for Passover and baby sister was sleeping in his mother's arms as they walked the dusty road. "I know she's getting heavy, Mother. Let me carry her awhile," Jesus said, and he gently lifted the sleeping baby from her arms.

Mary reached over to her son, and linked her arm in his. "Jesus, your sister is so small; she reminds me of the night you were born in Bethlehem," she said with a smile. "You were only a few hours old when a little shepherd boy came running breathlessly into the stable and nearly tumbled into my lap! He was waving his arms in the air and shouting in a whisper, 'We were just out there minding our sheep when an angel appeared out of nowhere! I was so scared! But the angel told us to come to this stable! So we took off running and now we're here to see the baby!'"

"Jesus," his mother said, "you were brand new, so tiny, and wrapped snuggly in your blanket on clean, fresh hay. The other shepherds, who had been outside watching, politely tiptoed in. I'll never forget the words of the older shepherd as he dropped to his knees next to the manger where you were sleeping. His tears ran into his beard and he said in his old raspy voice, 'Ooooh, here is the one we've been waiting for! And isn't he one perfect boy!'"

Jesus' mother never got tired of telling that story and he never got tired of hearing it. As they walked side-by-side she squeezed his arm a little tighter and said, "My son, you're growing up."

And that night….

Outside the gates of Jerusalem, the campfires had been set.
All the families had settled down and the night was quiet.
Jesus looked up at the millions of stars twinkling in the clear
black sky. He was thinking about his mother and how she
loved and cared for him! Then he spoke softly to his
Heavenly Father, "Thank you Father, for the love of my mother.
Thank you for giving me a good earthly father. Thank you for all
the ways you love me."

Then he turned on his side, shoulder and hip adjusting to the
hard ground, and he pulled the blanket up close to his face.
In the stillness of the cool, starry night and with a peaceful heart,
his breath became slow and even. Jesus felt a touch of breeze
against his cheek and his last thought before falling asleep was,
"Father, you are always with me."

That night, twelve-year-old Jesus dreamed he was sitting in the
big temple in Jerusalem listening to many teachers and answering
their questions. And his Father in Heaven was well pleased.

And just like you
As children do,
Jesus grew!

About the Author:

Kathy Samuels has published devotions in *God So Loved the World...That He Created Chocolate*. She received her master's degree in Creative Arts in Education from Lesley University in Cambridge, MA and retired from teaching at the elementary level after twenty-five years. She has taught children's Sunday school, was a MOP's mentor for seven years, continues to teach women's bible studies and has led women's ministries in her church. She is married to Roger and they have been blessed with five married children and eleven grandchildren. Born and raised in Pueblo, Colorado, she enjoys time at their cabin in the mountains of Colorado.

About the Illustrator:

Richard L. Marks is an artist, teacher, and muralist, living in Kiowa, Colorado with his wife Jessicca and daughter, Sarah. He also has two grown children, Josh and Jen. Richard worked as a Creative Director for Rocky Mountain Media for 15 years and has owned and operated Richard L. Marks Studios since 1997. He has won numerous awards for illustration and design and has many high profile clients to his credit. The last two years Richard has also been teaching art at Legacy Academy in Elizabeth, Colorado.

Selected Scripture for Corresponding Pages in One Perfect Boy

MARY AND BABY JESUS
Joseph was obedient and took Mary and Jesus to Egypt.
Matthew 2:13-15

CATCHING RAINDROPS
Jesus lived in Nazareth
Luke 1:26-28 , Matthew 2:19-23, Luke 4:16

Jesus had brothers.
Galatians 1:19, Matthew 13:55

Jesus spoke of a hen protecting her chicks.
Luke 13:34

When God the Father spoke from Heaven, Jesus heard him.
John 12:28-29

IN THE CARPENTER SHOP
Joseph took Mary to be his wife after the angel spoke to
him about her Divine pregnancy.
Matthew 1:18-25

Joseph was a carpenter.
Matthew 13:55

**The Torah is the first five books of the bible, beginning with
Genesis.*

PRUNING GRAPEVINES
Jesus spoke about planting and pruning.
Matthew 13:18-23, John 15:1-8

Almond trees grow in Israel.
Jeremiah 1:11

NIGHT ON A HILL
The Jewish people observed the Passover every year out of
obedience to God.
Exodus 12:21-27, Luke 2:41

Jesus taught his disciples that they were like the lights of a city on a hill.
Matthew 5:102, 5:14-16, Isaiah 2:5

PLAYING WITH CHILDREN
Jesus healed a man blind from birth.
John 9:1-17, 35-38

UNDER A TREE
Jesus often went to be alone to pray.
Matthew 14:13, 26:42, Mark 1:35, Luke 6:12,

Jesus used birds in a lesson.
Matthew 6:26-27

Jesus said, "Don't be afraid".
Matthew 14:27, Revelation 1:17

FINDING A LOST LAMB
Jesus used shepherds and sheep in his teaching.
Psalm 23:1-3, Matthew 18:12-14, Luke 15:4-7, John 10:25-30

AT THE SEA
Jesus had brothers and sisters.
Matthew 13:55-56

Jesus asked James and John to follow him. These fishermen became
his apostles. John wrote the book of John, 1st , 2nd , and 3rd John, and
Revelation.
Matthew 4:21-22, Matthew 10:2-4

A LIGHTNING STORM
Jesus is asked if he is a king.
John 18:33-37

Jesus called James and John "Sons of Thunder".
Mark 3:17

Perhaps Jesus sang.
Psalm 100:1-2, 144:9, Isaiah 12:6

JESUS HOLDS HIS SISTER
Jesus loved little children.
Mark 10:13-16

Jesus was the Son of God and the son of Mary. He was born in Bethlehem.
Matthew 1:18-25, Luke 1:1-56, Luke 2:1-20

Jesus was with God "In the beginning". He was God. He was called "the Word". He created everything.
John 1:1-5

Jesus was the only perfect One.
Hebrews 4:15

JESUS PRAYS
Jesus will reveal our hearts.
Luke 2:34-35

God the Father was pleased with his Son, Jesus. He loved him. Jesus was given to us for a purpose.
Matthew 3:17, John 3:16-17, John 14:6, Luke 3:22

God the Father was always with Jesus.
Matthew 26:53-54, 28:20

Jesus met with religious leaders in the Temple in Jerusalem when he was only twelve years old.
Luke 2:41-51

The Word became human and lived with us on earth.
John 1:14

Jesus was a child. He grew in wisdom and in height.
Luke 2:52

CONCLUSION
Keep your eyes on Jesus. Always. He loves you more than you can ask or imagine.
Hebrews 12:1-3, Ephesians 3:14-21